TRICK OR TREAT

CRYSTAL NORTH

For those who know the truth.

xoxo

CHAPTER ONE

The ringing of the bell has me hurrying to finish lighting the last candle. I knock off the lights, give the room a quick once over, and decide everything looks perfect. A quick glance in the mirror on the way past has me straightening my cat's ears headband on top of my long curly dark hair and readjusting the zip on my costume to show just the right amount of cleavage. I smile brightly and throw open the door to welcome my guests.

"Trick or treat!" The cry goes up and instead of facing my three undeniably gorgeous and smoking hot best friends, there's a group of about twelve trick-or-treaters stood on my doorstep in a myriad of costumes. I keep the smile plastered on my face, though it's a little more strained now, and shove the bowl of candy from the side towards them. Eager grabby little hands reach out and plunder the bowl leaving it half empty already.

Just as I'm about to close the door once I've waved them off from the driveway, three pairs of hands reach out and grab me from behind. Pulling me backwards off the doorstep, I scream until a calloused hand clamps over my mouth and my back meets with a rock hard body, then I relax. It's just Jasper.

"Aww, why did you stop screaming?" A voice to my left pouts. Sterling.

"Because no kidnappers, murderers or bad guys have bodies this good" I laugh, wiggling against Jasper a little. He's still got me clamped against his chest so my pvc clad catsuit ass rubs against his crotch.

"Naughty," he whispers in my ear, making delicious shivers run down my spine. "I could really make you scream, you know." Jasper's already low molten chocolate voice drops to a purr and I'm instantly wet between my thighs. I try to wiggle free and bump against his crotch again, loving how his cock has already started to stir to life. Obviously the costume was a good idea, even if it means sweating all night.

"You should have seen your face Ruri, when you opened the door to the kids not us!" A third voice, from my right laughs. Onyx.

"Guys," I pout. "Don't tease! Come in before we get more pesky candy stealers. I don't want to share."

Jasper drops his arms so that I'm free, and I step into the house to welcome them in. As each of my three best friends - and lifelong secret crushes - passes me by they kiss me on the cheek and wish me a Happy Hallo-birthday-ween. It's silly, but they've been doing it every year since I turned ten, when I moved to their neighbourhood and made friends with them. I didn't think that more than a decade later we'd be doing much the same thing, but there's nowhere I'd rather be.

"Go through to the den guys. I'm just going to fill up the candy." I tell them as they trail past. They don't exactly need telling where to go; they treat this place like a second home.

"Leave it on the doorstep," Sterling calls to me.

"What? Why?" I ask in confusion.

"Because we have a shit-ton of scary movies to get through and you don't want to be getting up every five seconds to open the door. Kids are annoying as fuck. Don't let them spoil the party."

I have to admit, he kind of has a point. If I disable the doorbell and leave the candy on the doorstep with a sign saying to help yourself, our evening will be a lot more fun uninterrupted. So I do as he suggested, closing the door and grabbing some beers on my way through the kitchen, before joining them in the den.

Sterling and Jasper have already made themselves comfortable on the couch, leaving a tiny gap between them that I'll never fit in, despite them patting the spot and begging me to join them. Onyx is putting the first film in.

"Ugh, do I even want to know what films you've chosen tonight?" I whine.

"You know Ruri, for someone with a Halloween birthday, you're really boring." Ouch. I try not to let it show how much Onyx's words sting, but really is there anything worse than being called boring?

"I don't see how not liking scary films makes me boring!" I retort.

"It's not just the films. You're finally twenty-one, why are you spending your birthday inside doing what you always do? I thought you'd want to do something special!" He pushes.

"This is special, to me. I hardly get to see you guys anymore since you're all so busy with work, and special is getting to do the things I love with the people I love. So for one night, I want to do just that."

"But you don't love it," Onyx insists. The room is tense now, the other two guys sitting stone still on the sofa, scared to move or interrupt this... conversation? Fight? Argument?

"I may not love the scary films, but I love the company and this is how I want to spend my birthday. If you have something better to do, you can go. No one is forcing you to spend time with boring old me."

"Aww babe..." Sterling starts to comfort me when Onyx doesn't say anything, but Jasper's arms once again wrap around me and pull me into his lap. I put my feet up on the tiny gap between him and Sterling, and snuggle into his chest.

"Just play the film." Sterling tells Onyx shortly. I can't work out if he's also pissed to be here spending Halloween with me how we always do, or if he's annoyed by Onyx upsetting me. Onyx grumbles but doesn't say anything audible and so we start the movie and I silently pass out the beers, feeling a lot more deflated than I was twenty minutes ago.

CHAPTER TWO

When the first movie ends, Onyx waits before lining up the next one. We agree to stop and have some drinks and some snacks before continuing. Everything is laid out on the coffee table that I've pushed to one side and so Jasper gets up from the couch to line up the shots. I rarely drink much but I know it's futile to refuse tonight. It is my twenty-first after all, and part of my is still smarting from the 'boring' comment.

"You ready, Ru?" Jasper calls. We all get up and walk over to the table to join him, kneeling down around the edge where an insane amount of drinks have been poured. "So tonight I thought we'd play a few Halloween-style games, starting with Apple Bobbing Trick-or-Treat!"

"I don't see any apples," I tell him, ignoring the fact that he seems to have mashed two games into one.

"The shots are apple flavoured," he replies, "and you're not allowed to use your hands to drink them. Sterl? Do the honours for me?" Before I can process what he's just said, Sterling has moved behind me, captured my wrists in his huge hands, and pulled them gently behind my back.

Something soft and silky wraps around them and a moment later when he lets go, I realise I'm bound and unable to move.

Instantly my nipples harden and my pupils dilate. Being tied up by Sterl, by any of these guys, has been a fantasy of mine for more years than I'd care to admit. Although, this wasn't exactly what I had in mind.

"Okay!" I beam in a desperate attempt to hide my excitement from them. "Let's do this. Is it a race? Are you joining me?"

"Onyx will go head to head with you. If you beat him, you win a prize. That's the treat."

"Okay and what if he wins?"

"You get a trick. You'll see." Jasper grins at me wickedly and I gulp. There's no way I'm losing to Onyx after his boring comment.

"Ok, get ready you two... three, two, one..."

I start before he yells go. Kneeling up, I bend at the waist and clamp my teeth around the first shot glass. I straighten, tip my head back and swallow the sour apple concoction down in one. Returning for the next, I drop the empty glass from my mouth and race on, repeating until there's just one shot left and sour apple liqueur is trailing down from my mouth between my breasts. I'm a sticky mess but determined to...

"And stop! We have a winner!" Jasper cries. Shit. I lost. Fuck it, I think to myself, and down the last shot anyway. A quick peek at Onyx shows he's in a similar state to me, but looks shocked that I finished and almost beat him. "That was pretty close." Jasper confirms. "But, sorry Ru, you lost." Ugh tell me something I didn't know already.

"Okay, so what does he win?" I ask. "And can I get my arms untied now?"

"No point," Sterling says. "No arms allowed in the next game either."

"What do you want as your prize, Onyx?" I demand.

"You." He smirks. I stare at him in disbelief, refusing to get my hopes up even as my heart rate spikes and my temperature soars. He can't mean what I'm thinking. There's no way.

A brief look from Onyx to Jasper to Sterling gives nothing away. These guys all have excellent poker faces. No one speaks. And I swallow nervously.

"What did you have in mind?" I ask, failing to hide the nervous tremor in my voice.

"Oh, I think I can think of a few things, but I'll start with tidying you up." Onyx grins at me. "Sterl? My hands please?" Sterling gets to his feet and unties Onyx's hands from behind his back.

Onyx then crawls the couple of feet space between us while I stay frozen to the spot. I'm barely breathing and when he gets close enough that our knees touch and I smell his spicy scent, the alcohol hits and I feel dizzy and faint.

With my hands still tied behind my back, there's nothing I can do as Onyx threads his fingers through my loose hair and uses his grip to tilt my head to the side and away from him, exposing my long neck with the apple dribble running down. He leans in close and starts at the base of my throat, using his tongue to trace its leisurely way back up my neck towards my lips, removing all trace of the liquor as he goes.

I hold my breath and bite my lip to keep from moaning, but my pulse flutters erratically in my neck and Onyx chuckles. Bastard. He knows exactly what he's doing to me. But why? Why is he doing this? He ends his seductive ascent by licking the dribble of apple from the corner of my mouth, then kisses me lightly on the lips. It takes everything I have to not react, when all I want to do is devour his mouth.

Hell, who am I kidding? I want to do a hell of a lot more than that!

CHAPTER THREE

"Fuck, that's hot." Jasper grunts.

"Yeah, but you missed a bit man," Sterling points to where the shots had trickled down between my breasts and I heat as all three pairs of eyes swivel to my chest.

"I didn't want to push my luck." Onyx replies, but I don't know what he means. He leaves the room without another word.

"Shall we play another game?" Jasper says eagerly.

"Sure," I reply in a breathless whisper. "What's next?"

"Sterling? I think the next game is yours."

Sterling gets to his feet and helps me to mine. He leads me from the den to the kitchen, and I see what Onyx was doing after he left. Sugared ring donuts hang from the beam in the kitchen and I sigh. I know this game, and I suck at it.

"Looks like Ru's already admitting defeat one this one!" Sterling crows. He has such a big mouth; I'd never stand a chance against him in an eating contest. Still, I'm not about to give in.

"Never!" I cry, shouldering him out of the way and

taking up my place behind the first donut. "How many do we have to eat?"

"Just one," Jasper replies with a smirk. It seems too easy. "But no licking your lips!" Damn it! I knew there'd be a catch. I pout, lick my lips ready to begin, and mentally steel myself to win this one.

"On your marks...get set..." Jasper calls out, but Sterling jumps ahead and takes a massive bite out of his donut.

"Cheat!" I cry.

"Go!" Jasper yells.

"But he cheated!" I protest.

"And he's winning! Chop chop Ru! You're losing." Jasper teases.

I spin back to my donut and race to catch up but I know it's futile. Sugar coats half my face and drops in my eyes but with my hands tied, there's nothing I can do about it. Thank god there's not jam in these; I'd be a mess.

"And stop!" Jasper calls out. I don't finish my donut. "Tut-tut, Ru. I feel like you're not even trying." He mock-scolds me.

"Sterling cheated." I sulk, even though I know it's pointless.

"Now, now, don't be a sore loser," Onyx chides me. He comes to stand behind me, pressing his firm chiselled body against me, arms encircling my waist so that I can't breathe or think straight. Sterling spins and grins at me, and suddenly I'm the filling of a fantasy sandwich. Dry mouth, wet down south, I stare and tremble, unable to react.

"Wh... what do you... what are you doing?" I stammer.

"Claiming my prize," Sterling replies a moment before his lips capture mine in a perfectly soft kiss. Sadly, it's over before it begins and then he's licking the sugar from around my mouth. This time I can't stop the whimper that escapes me. Damn he's good with his tongue. All too soon he stops though and I huff in annoyance.

"If we're just going to spend the night licking me, I can think of better places you could start," I grumble in frustration. Jasper laughs uproariously and Sterling looks shocked at my suggestive innuendo. I can't see Onyx but I'm pretty sure the shaking I can feel behind me is his silent laughter. "Can you untie me now? My arms ache and I have sugar in my eyes," I complain.

Onyx springs into action and frees me, but before I can move, he spins me to face him and gently brushes the sugar from my lashes. A quick inspection shows my eyes are all clear, so his hands move to my shoulders where he gently rubs the aches away.

After that, there's a quick game of real apple bobbing - which I win and which results in Sterling teasing me that I look good wet. If only he knew. Turning back to the den, I declare it's time for another drink. Or ten. I don't know what these guys are playing at tonight, but they've got me all kinds of messed up.

"Truth or dare?" Jasper pounces as soon as we sit down.

"Truth." I don't hesitate but I laugh. "Seriously though, after all this time there can't be anything you guys don't know about me!" I down the shots that Sterling lined up for me and chase the awful taste away with another coke. Much better.

"I'm sure we'll think of something original," Jasper adds with a wink. "Tell me, Ru, which of us do you fancy?"

"At one time or another, probably all three of you," I laugh but to my ears it sounds forced.

"Yeah but I didn't ask which of us you fancied, I asked which of us you fancy."

"Semantics. I answered your question. Your turn. Truth or dare?" I hurriedly move on, skirting the question.

"Dare." He states emphatically.

"I dare you to...erm..." I falter. God, this is another game I'm crap at. "Sterl? Help me?"

"I dare you to kiss Ruri," he supplies helpfully.

"No!" I cry at the same time as Jasper agrees "Done!"

He turns to me on the sofa and grins wickedly at me. As butterflies riot in my stomach, I can't help but return his smile. Jasper is absolutely gorgeous. All the guys are. But there's something mesmerising about his caramel skin, long curly dark mahogany locks and eyes as dark and warm as espresso. His twinkle is contagious.

"You ready, Ru?" He asks softly, all joking gone from his face. I nod, at a loss for words.

The last thing he says to me before our lips touch is "I've waited a long time for this."

CHAPTER FOUR

His kiss makes my head spin. What did his last words mean? I'm so confused for a moment, but then distracted as all thoughts fly out of my head with his deepening kiss. If everything about Jasper reminds me of caramel and chocolate, his kiss is no exception. I've got such a sweet tooth that I could happily spend a lifetime drowning in his kisses. Our tongues tangle in a dance that I've been dreaming of for years. Without breaking the kiss, he grabs my hips and slides me onto his lap so that I'm straddling him.

It's at about the moment when I grind down onto his hardening erection that throats clear behind us and I reluctantly pull away from him, embarrassed. He grins at me sheepishly and pulls me back to his chest to whisper in my ear "totally worth it", which makes me blush even more.

"The dare was to kiss, not to bloody maul her." Onyx grumbles.

"I liked it," I state defiantly at Onyx who's glowering at me. "Who's next?" I ask and Sterling's mouth falls agape. "I meant, for truth or dare," I say laughing, "but I can guess what you might want your dare to be."

"You go. Dare." Onyx tells me.

"Don't I get to choose?" I frown.

"You picked truth last time, so it's dare this time." His tone is not to be messed with, but I've never been one to listen where Onyx is concerned. Of all the guys he's the one I fight with the most. Sometimes he just rubs me up the wrong way, and despite it being my birthday, tonight seems to be one of those nights.

"When did those rules come into play?" I ask.

"When you grew up. When you insisted you're not boring. When you dodged the last truth question."

"Fine! Ask me anything!" I cry. "I won't dodge this time."

"Fine." Onyx crossed his arms in defiance and stares at me. "Which one of us do you masterbate over?"

"I'll take the dare." I grind out. There's no way I'm answering a truth if that's what he's going to ask!

When he smirks at me, as if he knew that would be my reaction, my hackles rise. "I'll do your dare, but the truth you can have for free. All of you. I fancy all of you and I..." I falter, take a deep breath and begin again, refusing to give him the satisfaction, "masterbate over all of you. Frequently." Then, to the stunned silence of the room, I raise my chin and ask, "Now what's my dare?"

"I dare you to mas-" Onyx begins.

"I dare you to kiss me!" Sterling jumps in. Thank Christ.

"No problem," I smile at him. I'm absolutely relieved that Sterling jumped to my rescue, and I'm seriously annoyed at Onyx. I have no clue what his problem is tonight, but I do know that I want to wind him up like he's doing to me. So I climb off Jasper's lap and slink towards

Sterling as sexily as possible. I know that I look good in my all-in-one bodysuit and that the guys aren't used to seeing me dressed up, let alone dressed this sexy. The feeling of three sets of eyes watching my every move is powerful and heady.

When I reach Sterling sat in the armchair, I straddle his lap, loop my arms around his neck and take a moment to study him. In the low candlelight, his olive skin glows and his light ocean eyes glisten with mischief and... arousal? He has a neat and tidy five o'clock shadow that really highlights his chiselled facial features and strong jawline. His short brown hair runs a little longer in the front and spikes upwards with no product. I've always loved to run my fingers through his silky soft locks and now is no exception. Doing so brings my body flush against his. His sudden intake of breath has me looking down and I notice that my breasts are pushed up against his chin. He's staring right at my chest and so with one hand I reach down and slowly lower the zip a little more. When his eyes threaten to bulge out of his head, I chuckle and use one finger to lift his chin so that he meets my gaze.

"I'm up here," I tell him huskily, lowering my lips to meet his before he can say anything. I kiss him passionately, using his gasp of surprise to slip my tongue in past his defences. His strong arms wrap around me and his huge hands palm my ass and pull me against his hardness. Every line and cut ridge of his body rubs against me and I moan into his mouth. I need more friction. I need more...every-thing. I try my best to convey this message to him through our kiss. From the way he grinds me back and forth on his lap, I'd say he received my message loud and clear.

"Enough!" Onyx barks. It takes a moment for his words

to sink in, and when I break away from Sterling, it's just in time to see Onyx storming out of the room.

Shit.

CHAPTER FIVE

I scramble off Sterling's lap and look from him to Jasper, silently asking for guidance.

"Go talk to him, Ruri," Jasper tells me. Sterling just groans and adjusts his sizeable hard-on beneath his jeans. Damn. I'd much rather stay and help him with that. "When you come back, bring Onyx with you and we'll give you your birthday present."

My face must give away my excitement or my naughty thoughts or something because Jasper laughs and chides me, "dirty girl, not that" and I pout as Sterling groans again.

I turn to him and see that he still has his hands down his jeans. I wag my finger at him playfully and tell him, "Hands off! I want that for my birthday." I blow him a kiss as he runs his free hand through his hair in frustration and then turn on my heel to leave.

Onyx is out in the kitchen, downing a beer. I approach him cautiously, unsure of what to say to him now. I don't know what's up with him; he seems to have been in a strange mood all night.

"You okay?" Is the lame question I settle on. His empty

beer bottle meets the empty sink with a loud clatter. Thankfully, it doesn't break. Onyx doesn't say anything. "I'll take that as a no then, On." I whisper. Still, he doesn't reply and annoyance flares in my veins. "On! You're ruining my birthday. Whatever is up, spit it out would you!?"

I watch as Onyx runs his hands through his messy dark hair and sighs, his muscles rippling under his grey tee. He's clearly agitated and not himself tonight, and I want to know why. I stare up at his blue eyes that are too dark, too much, against his pale skin, and note the expression there. I can only describe it as tortured. He's always had that delicious bad boy appeal going on, but tonight everything about him just seems so much...*more*.

"On? What's..."

Before I can finish, Onyx growls in warning and it's the only sign I have of what's coming. Unfortunately, my brain is too slow to realise what's going on and in two short strides Onyx has crossed the room, crashed into me and pushed me up against the wall.

"You're driving me crazy, Ru," he murmurs against me. Every inch of his body is flush with mine. Every bump, groove, ridge, and bulge presses into me intimately. I've never been this close to Onyx before. There's nothing soft or forgiving about him, but damn, if he doesn't make my body dance and sing at his touch.

"What do you mean?"

"You." He bites, moving his arms to either side of my head, caging me in and using his hips to pin me in place. "You're too fucking... innocent. I can't stand it." The size-able erection straining against my hot core belies his words.

"Have you seen what I'm wearing? I hardly think it counts as innocent." I scoff.

"It's a costume Ru, it's not who you really are." He sounds sad to say it.

"Really? And does someone who's innocent spend the best part of a decade fantasising over their best friend?" I challenge. When I correct that statement to 'best friends', with a heavy emphasis on the 's', Onyx hisses, his nose flares and his erection jerks against me. I tease its outline through his jeans. "Am I so innocent that I just admitted to masterbating over the three of you? I've been doing it for years."

"Ru, don't push me." He warns. But where would be the fun in that?

"If I were so innocent, would everything that's happened tonight have me absolutely...dripping?" I tease in a breathless whisper.

Something in Onyx snaps. In a split second his body is gone from mine - I feel the absence of his heat - and then it's back, slamming against me with such force that my breath is stolen from me. Before I can recover, Onyx's lips are on me in the most brutally punishing kiss I've ever experienced in my life. His hands encircle my slim wrists and drag them above my head, where he locks them in one of his large hands, freeing the other to trail down my arm and the side of my breast until it comes to rest on my zipper.

I squirm against him, loving that I can't move, relishing the way his cock twitches as I futilely struggle against him. I want to meet Onyx stroke for stroke, but he won't allow it; he dominates our kiss, controls our whole interaction. Without pausing from his plundering kiss, he yanks my zipper down with force then roughly grabs my bare breast. The nipple is already harder than glass, but when he starts to twist and tug it, sending brutal spikes of pleasure down to my pussy, it turns to fucking diamond. I try to beg him - for more, not to stop - but he bites my lip to swallow my pleas.

When his hand thrusts between my thighs, it's Onyx that breaks the kiss with a sigh. "You're fucking soaked, Ru," he sighs.

"Nope, I'm not. I'm far too innocent for that, remember?" I can't help but give him sass, but that earns me a sharp bite on my nipple and I yelp. Unfortunately, wetness floods me at the same time and Onyx's grin tells me that he felt it.

His fingers start a slow caress of my folds, leisurely, like he has all the time in the world. I jerk my hips towards him to encourage him to go faster but he chuckles and slows even more. I whimper in frustration and he grins. Bastard. Eventually though, he dips a finger inside and my muscles immediately seize it and clamp down greedily on him. He slowly pumps in and out of me, but I need more.

"Kiss me," I demand, but it comes out more like a plea.

"Oh no," Onyx insists. "I'd much rather watch." He continues to thrust his finger into my wetness, slowly adding another and filling me. "Fuck you're tight."

"Must...be..." I gasp out. Shit, how can something so torturously slow feel so good? "All that...innocence." I quip, earning me another savage nip on the other nipple this time.

My stupid mouth!

Somehow, despite the blood roaring in my ears, I make out the sounds of a group of trick-or-treaters making their way down the drive. They'll be at the door any moment - inches away from us. My eyes widen in horror at the same moment Onyx's darken. Then they alight with challenge and determination.

CHAPTER SIX

"I think it's time you came now, don't you?" He purrs wickedly in my ear. I frantically shake my head but he doesn't listen. "You wanted more, right?" He teases.

I desperately beg him to stop but he pays me no mind. I'm still trapped beneath him, arms stretched high above my head, legs spread wide because of the way he's stood between them. I couldn't stop him even if I *really* wanted to.

Onyx shifts his fingers inside me so that his thrusts are shallower, faster. Instead of long hard strokes that mimic the promise of his cock, he curls his fingers to rub against that sweet spot. My knees buckle and I hate the smirk he gives me.

Outside, the trick-or-treaters have reached the door. I can hear them plundering the candy jar inches away from us, but it feels like I'm underwater, hearing everything from a hazy distance.

"I don't know what to pick," one voice whines from outside.

"Just choose your fucking candy already!" I growl low through gritted teeth and Onyx laughs.

"Oh Ru, you're going to have to be quieter than that," he teases, grazing his thumb over my clit while internally his fingers continue to summon a genie.

The fucking tell-tale tingling starts in the soles of my feet and a tidal wave of heat surges up to my head. Everything tingles. Everything trembles. I desperately try to clamp my thighs together, but Onyx is having none of it. His eyes are practically dancing with sadistic mirth and desperately try to stave off my orgasm.

"It's no use, Ru." He tells me at the *exact* same moment my brain registers the *exact* same thought. Fuck. I'm so fucked.

I clamp my jaw closed and grit my teeth as I reach the crescendo. Every trembling muscle in my body goes taut. I suck in a deep shuddering breath then bite down so hard on my lip I taste blood.

"Tick, tock, tick, tock," the fucking bastard teases. I'm panting so hard now, I don't know how they can't hear me outside. A pitiful, anguished mewling sound breaks free of my lips but I'm too far gone to care.

"What was that?"

"Did you hear that?"

"It sounded like a kitty."

The voices from outside the door drift clearly through to us and Onyx laughs again.

"Not a kitty, just a gorgeous, tight pussy," he quietly corrects.

"Here kitty, kitty," the voices call.

"Come pussy, pussy," Onyx teases.

With an uncontrollable shout, the dam bursts and my orgasm floods Onyx's hand. My bones liquefy, my muscles turn to jelly. I sag against the wall, panting. Thank Christ he's holding me up.

"What was that?!" I voice from outside yells.

"This place is haunted!" Another panicked cry goes up.

"RUN!" Terrorised screams rent the air and Onyx laughs, removing his hand from my catsuit and bringing it to his lips. I watch in fascination as he licks my juices from fingers. A moment ago I was done, spent, but watching him enjoy my flavour has me burning to go again.

"That was…" I stammer, panting hard. I can barely catch my breath. Hell, I'm barely standing. Everything is still trembling from the aftershocks of my orgasm. It was the best orgasm of my life. Not that I'll be telling Onyx that; he has a big enough head already. I don't want to over-inflate it for him.

"Yeah." Onyx agrees, but I can already see the distance he's placing back between us in his eyes. Some of my shiny, happy glow fades a little as he physically steps back from me too.

"Look Ru," Onyx begins.My heart sinks. I would give anything right now for him to not finish that sentence. Nothing good ever came from a sentence that starts with 'look' - especially after sex.

"Ru?" His knitted brow draws my attention back to him. If my shiny had started to fade at the expression in his eyes, and my heart sank at his 'we need to talk' style 'look', ice-cold dread fills me with his next words…

"You need to choose."

My eyes widen in horror and I instinctively step towards him, but he avoids my touch.

"On, don't." I plead. I shake my head in denial. "Don't do this."

"You have to." He insists. I feel like he's ripping my gut

out. Why? Why now, after so many years of longing for this day, does he threaten to tear apart everything I ever dreamed of?

Because it's a dream of course, and dreams aren't meant to come true. Not really. What ever happened to the girl who got everything she ever wanted? Exactly.

I know he's right, I do, but I still can't choose.

"On, please." I beg, "I can't choose. You're all my best friends. I love you all. Please don't make me pick between you."

Onyx is completely impervious to my entreaties. His cold blue eyes are hardened like icebergs; every muscle in his body is tense and unyielding. He won't bend on this one.

"Choose, Ruri." I know he means business; he's back to using my full name. "Tonight."

"Come," he calls over his shoulder as he walks away from me without a backward glance. "You've got a birthday present to open."

I trail after him, absolutely miserable. The elation of my orgasm at Onyx's hand is long gone, washed away by the cold wave of Onyx's indifference towards me and what we just shared. I feel like tonight is the ultimate game of trick or treat, but whatever I choose, I just can't seem to win.

CHAPTER SEVEN

Miserably, I race upstairs to clean up and change. I'm too hot and bothered to stay in this stupid costume now. I slip into my lace cami and shorts set, but leave the cat's ears on. They're cute. Then I follow Onyx back into the den.

It's considerably darker than when we left and I realise that several of the candles have already burnt out. How long were we gone? Sterling has moved from the armchair I left him in and is back on the sofa beside Jasper. They've already started the next film, but I don't mind. Onyx has taken the armchair and is looking at me expectantly. Where do I sit? Will my decision send a message to Onyx about my choice?

"Come on, Ru." Jasper smiles at me and pats the small space between him and a Sterling. "Saved you a spot." I glance from him to Onyx, who's watching me. His face is impassive stone; it gives nothing away.

I slide onto the sofa between the two boys and they pause the movie.

"Can we give you your present now?" Jasper asks me.

"Yeah, you were gone ages," Sterling grumbles. "Was Onyx being a total twat?"

"Something like that," I murmur.

Jasper and Sterling laugh, but I don't dare look at Onyx's reaction. Instead, I focus on the small gift bag Jasper has dropped into my lap.

"Thank you." I smile at him.

"You haven't even opened it yet. Don't thank us; you might hate it."

"When have I ever hated anything you've given me?" Besides Onyx's edict, I think to myself. Yeah, that's one 'gift' I wasn't too keen on.

"Just open it, Ru."

I listen to him and focus fully on the parcel in my hands. It's an excellent distraction. From the bag I pull a small jewellery box which isn't wrapped, and I carefully prise the lid open.

Nestled inside, on a bed of black silk, is a stunning deep blue teardrop pendant. I can't see it in this light, but I know that it will be run through with ribbons and flecks of gold.

"It's Lapis..." Jasper begins to explain.

"Lazuli," I finish for him. "I know. After my namesake." Since the day we met, the guys had been fascinated by my unusual and exotic name, which means Lapis Lazuli in Japanese. My parents were crazy hippy travellers with a love for all things shiny it would seem. Imagine our joy, aged ten, when we discovered that the four of us were bound by gemstone names. It was a sign we were meant to be best friends forever. Or so we naively thought back then.

"I love it, thank you." I breathe, one foot still trapped half in the past.

"Are you sure?" Jasper worries. "Because if you don't like it, we can change it."

"No! I love it. I really do." I insist. "I was just thinking of the day we met." I smile, but it's bittersweet. Obviously we weren't those innocent children anymore, but I truly didn't think things had changed that much between us over the years, until tonight. Now Onyx's ultimatum weighed heavily on me like lead.

"Put it on," Onyx orders.

"Would you like to try it on?" Jasper asks, much more politely than Onyx.

"Absolutely," I tell Jasper with a smile. I slip the pendant from the box and open the chair. I hold it out to Jasper and ask him to do the honours. When he takes it from my grasp, I gently lift my curls up out for the way to bear my neck to him. He reaches around and gently fastens the chain around my neck and I let my curls drop.

The pendant is on a short chain - almost like a choker - and it nestles comfortably in the small hollow dip at the base of my throat.

"Perfect," this time Onyx's voice is much softer and when I meet his eyes, he's giving me a look that I can't decipher, but causes my stomach to flip. He starts the film again and I ask Sterling to pass me my drink. I need something to do with my shaking hands, something to hide behind.

"You okay, Ru?" Jasper asks me, his face full of concern. "You're shaking."

"I'm fine," I tell him.

"It's not that scary!" Sterling jokes, throwing his arm around my shoulders and pulling me into his chest. I curl my feet up to keep from toppling over and Jasper immediately pulls them into his lap. When he starts to massage my feet, I finally begin to relax.

It takes me a while for me to notice that Jasper is no

longer rubbing my feet. Instead, his hands have moved to my calves and are slowly working the tension away.

"What's up, Ru? You're all knotted up." Jasper has hit the nail on the head; my stomach is in knots, worrying about this stupid demand that Onyx has put over me. My stress always manifests in my muscles, every single one turning to stone.

Thankfully, I'm saved from having to answer him by Sterling's hands making their way to my shoulders. He kneads and as he agrees with Jasper about how tense I am, I can't stop the sultry moan that slides from my lips.

"Want us to make you feel good, Ru?" Jasper's molten chocolate tones wash over me and I nod.

"Trick or Treat?" Sterling asks me.

"Trick." Onyx calls out from across the room.

"Great choice, Ru, and you said that workout moving your lips at all." Sterling grins down at me and I sigh and close my eyes. I don't want to watch these guys torture me, but I also don't have the strength to tell them to stop.

"You see Ru," Sterling murmurs in my ear, his voice low with arousal. "I have an excellent party trick...would you like me to demonstrate it on you?" I nod.

"Excellent choice," Jasper adds.

I don't want to know. I'm just going to keep my eyes closed and hope for the best.

Sterling lowers me from his chest so that I'm lying with my head in his lap. I can feel his erection pressing into the side of my face. Don't think about it, I tell myself. I let my head fall the other way, away from Sterling, towards Onyx. If I was brave enough to open my eyes, I'd be able to see him. But I'm a coward, so I don't.

Jasper parts my legs a little and behind to stroke his calloused palms up and down the inside of my bare thighs. I think I should have kept the pvc on because it at least offered me some coverage, but his hands feel like velvet on my soft skin. His touch is steady, rhythmic, and I melt into it while Sterling slips the thin straps from my lace camisole down my shoulders. When my nipples pebble in the cool air, I know that I'm lying exposed before him, and I hold my breath in anticipation of what comes next.

CHAPTER EIGHT

I startle a little when Sterling's hands graze my shoulders. His touch is soft and gentle, but unexpected. He increases the pressure and continues to knead my shoulders once again.

"Relax Ru," he whispers to me, but it's easier said than done. Jasper is tracing patterns on my thighs with the tips of his fingers with an agonisingly light touch that makes me want to squirm and giggle at the same time. Sterling is just as distracting; with every pass of his hands over my shoulders, his hands are dipping lower and lower onto my chest so that his fingers graze my breasts.

I let out a contented sigh which seems to serve as some sort of green light to Sterling, who drops all pretence of massaging my shoulders and moves both of his hands to my full breasts. They already feel full and heavy from Onyx's earlier ministrations, but now I'm practically keening with need.

"Sterl..." I begin, but he cuts me off with a frustrating "Shh".

"My party trick is brilliant," he croons in my ear. "I can

make you come without going anywhere near that sweet little pussy of yours."

I cry out as he tugs hard in my nipples and lightning shoots to my core.

"Jesus, I can feel her heat through her shorts," Jasper announces to the whole room. Thank Christ he didn't say... "she smells fucking amazing." Too late. I cover my face with my hands, absolutely mortified, but unable to escape anywhere.

"She tastes fucking amazing too," Onyx calls out. That's it, I want the ground to swallow me up. It's the only way I'm getting out of here.

"Truth or dare, Ruri?" Onyx calls again.

"What?"

"Truth. Or. Dare." His voice takes on that no-nonsense tone that I always used to call his bastard voice. If I could bring myself to look at him I know I'd see the same expression mirrored in his eyes. But I don't dare; that look has always been my undoing.

"T-tr-truth," I cry as Sterling increases the intensity on my nipples. My arms fly to my sides and I arch my back up off his lap in a desperate attempt for some relief, but he just chuckles and Jasper helps push me back in my place.

"Did you enjoy yourself earlier in the kitchen, Ruri?" My eyes snap open and I stare at Onyx in disbelief. What is he doing? He fixes me with a firm stare that says I better tell the truth or I'll live to regret it. I gulp.

"Yes." I whisper.

"Ah, but which time? When you were playing games, or when I was playing with you?"

"Both." I barely manage to squeak out. Fuck, Sterling is distracting. And Jasper...Jasper's now tracing patterns on my thighs with his tongue. Fuck.

"Did you like cumming on my fingers, Ru? Have you been dreaming of it for years?"

"Yes! Yes!" I sob.

"Do you want to cum on my tongue?"

"Please!" I plead. I have no idea what I'm begging for. I'm seeing stars. I'm so close.

"Do you want me to bury my hard cock deep into your tight pussy until you milk it dry?"

An unholy scream tears from my throat as my orgasm rips through my body. My eyes never leave Onyx the whole time. It may have been Sterling and Jasper who were touching me, but there's no doubt in my mind that it was Onyx's words which made me come undone. I've always been drawn to him, powerless to stop the strange pull. He's always held power over me that I'm unable to fight. It's why I challenge him so much in other areas; a desperate attempt to gain some ground with him.

I lie there, heaving, and this time no one in the room can miss the scent of my orgasm filling the air. I'm too exhausted to care. I lie back in Sterling's lap as he grins down at me and I give him a weak but thankful smile in return.

"I've been to loads of parties with you guys, how come I've never seen that trick before?" I ask and they all laugh.

"Can we give you your treat now?" Jasper asks.

"I thought that was a treat," I reply. I'm honestly pretty sated right now.

"Oh Ru, we're just getting started, silly." Jasper reaches up to grip the edge of my shorts, and with Sterling's help to lift my ass, he's able to easily slide them down my thighs and off. Jasper removes the lace cami that's bunched up and forgotten around my waist.

And then I'm naked. In front of three guys. Three fully clothed guys who are my closest friends in the world. I should be mortified, but their heated gazes make me feel empowered. They want this as much as I do.

Jasper flips me over so that I'm on all fours, and I hear him scrambling behind me to remove his clothes as Sterling rips off his shirt, unbuttons his jeans and slides them down just enough for his cock to spring free. For a moment, I'm completely distracted by the rippling muscles on his abdomen. I want to run my tongue over every dip and ridge. But then my gaze comes to land on his cock and my mouth waters at the sight of the bead of pre-cum nestled at the tip.

"Go on Ru." Sterling encourages, "You know you want to taste."

I bite my lip but hesitate, desperate for a taste. I don't know how we got here, but it's a dream come true. I lean forward slowly and bend to take a taste. My tongue flicks out and steals the droplet on his slit. An explosion of salty flavour burst on my tongue and I swallow back a greedy groan, desperate to devour him whole. My eyes snap to Onyx, who's watching intently and lock onto his. I wrap my full lips around the tip of Sterling's cock and slide slowly down to the base, eyeballing Onyx the whole time, daring him to call me boring now. The flare of his nostrils is the only giveaway that he's affected by my actions.

Satisfied, I turn back to Sterling's long cock and give it my full attention. I want to go to slow, to tease him, to savour it, but I can't. I'm too greedy, too needy. Instead, I begin to bob enthusiastically up and down his shaft, slurping and messily devouring his cock like it's my last meal on earth. I only pause when Jasper startles me by entering me slowly from behind. His cock feels thicker than Sterling's but maybe a touch shorter. It's hard to tell. It's hard to concentrate or think or...

"Oh god," I groan, Sterling's cock slipping from my lips,

my eyes rolling back in my head as Jasper hits my sweet spot at the same time as rubbing my too-sensitive clit.

Holy shit! Just like that I'm being spit roast. It's a fucking dream come true. Completely distracted, there's little I can do to pleasure Sterling. I'm just kind of hanging on for the ride while Jasper pounds into me. He's pummelling me so hard I'm in danger of choking so I switch to sucking Sterling's tip and using my hands to give him pleasure instead.

Once again, I feel the heat of Onyx's gaze on my bare skin, and I find him still watching me intently.

"On, please," I beg, my hand reaching out imploringly. "Join us."

CHAPTER NINE

I hold my breath while I wait for Onyx's reaction. For a moment he doesn't respond or react. I really worry that he's going to refuse. Then suddenly he gets to his feet and gruffly tells the other two to move.

In a few short strides he reaches me on the couch, wraps one strong arm around my waist and lifts me up over the arm of the sofa. He bends me over it so that my ass is high in the air and I have to stand on tip-toes to keep my balance. Sterling comes closer and kneels on the sofa in front of me so that I can continue sucking him, Jasper standing along-side him so that I can pleasure him with a simple turn of my head.

"Stop!" Onyx barks and I freeze.

"Dude!" Sterling moans. "What the fuck?"

"I want her to focus on what I'm giving her. Watch."

To my complete and utter dismay, Jasper and Sterling move away from me and take their seats to watch the show. I grumble to myself about going off some people quickly while giving them both a dirty look. He might be to blame, but I'm not about to sass Onyx; he might not give me what I'm craving.

Onyx doesn't speak, just grips my hips to position me exactly where he wants me, and lines up his ready and waiting cock at my entrance. Unlike Jasper, Onyx doesn't gently enter me. He slams into me, balls deep, causing me to cry out.

"See? Told you we would make you scream." Jasper smirks at me.

"Er, I think you'll find you said you could make me scream." I gasp out between Onyx's thrusts. He's relentless. "Could, not would. You, not Onyx!"

"Challenge accepted, Ru," Sterling winks at me. "Wait til round two!"

I have no comeback to that as a resounding slap fills the room.

"Fuck!" I scream, then groan as Onyx rubs my tender ass that he's just spanked. God that feels good. I push back and wiggle my ass, trying to tempt him to do it again. It doesn't work.

Instead, Onyx grabs my hips in a bruising grip and starts to pound into me at high speed. It's brutal and punishing; his cock is so thick *and* long. It's hard to take, painfully delicious, but oh-so-good. After a moment he moves his right hand to my back and presses down hard so that I'm unable to squirm against him. His other hand snakes around to grip my throat.

I love the way he places his strong hand around my neck, almost as much as the squeeze he gives my throat, causing a gush of wetness to flood me. I groan and lean into it, wanting more and he chuckles.

"Nope, Ru, this is for me." He tells me. I don't know what he hopes to achieve with his words, but my pussy doesn't get the message. Instead, it clenches tightly around him and tries to kill him hard. My orgasm - another I didn't think possible - is just out of reach, but as he continues to spank me and squeeze me and roughly handle me, I can feel its imminence.

"On, please," I beg him. I just need...something. One small thing to take me over the edge. It's just out of reach like the amazing dream you half remember when you wake, but desperately try to chase.

His thrusts reach fever pitch and I instantly know three things: he's about to cum; there's no way I could have pleasured Jasp and Sterl with this punishing fuck; and I'm going to be sore tomorrow. Hell, I'm already sore!

Onyx reaches round with his right hand and roughly rubs my clit. There's no finesse or care being taken; this is as frantic as his final thrusts. It works though; my pussy clenches and I tremble. It's the hard pinch to my clit that makes me snap.

Without caring who hears, I scream and instantly strong spasms take over my pussy. I feel Onyx's hot seed spilling inside me and the realisation that I've made him come undone drills my orgasm onward. I milk every last drop of his cum until he stops thrusting. Spent, he collapses on me for a moment, his breathless pants heaving his chest firmly against my clammy back.

"Did you like that, Ruri?" Onyx asks a couple of minutes later, lifting himself up off my back and gently running a hand down my still-tingling spine. His touch is almost tender and I revel in it.

I don't have the energy to move or speak, but I do manage a feeble nod. I squeak in disbelief when Onyx's still-hard cock swell inside me again. Fuck. How is that even possible?

"Was it everything you dreamed of?"

"More," I choke out.

"Good..." he pulls out and I instantly feel bereft, making a small sound of protest. "Because it's time for you to choose."

CHAPTER TEN

"Wh-what?" I blink still processing the loss of warmth from Onyx's body. What did he just say?

"You need to choose, Ruri." Onyx repeats. "What do you want? Who do you want? Pick today. Now."

My stomach drops faster than a roller coaster free fall. The shiny happy glow evaporates instantly. Something white-hot - shame and embarrassment? - burns through my body chasing away the final tingles of pleasure.

"What the fuck dude?" Sterling shouts at Onyx and they start to bicker, leaving me forgotten about.

I feel ridiculous still bent over the arm of the chair, ass in the air, feet barely reaching the ground. I scramble to right myself and then desperately look around for some-thing to cover up with. I spy Sterling's tee on the back of the sofa and quickly snag it and pull it over my head. I'm always stealing his clothes and he's always moaning that I put "lady bumps" in them.

I sit on the sofa and pull my knees up against my chest, stretching the t-shirt down over them so that I'm cocooned.

I've made myself as small as possible, shrinking back into the far corner of the sofa, wishing it would swallow me.

The arguing intensifies and the noise level rises, drawing my attention to the three guys standing in the centre of the room. Jasper and Sterling are still undressed, Onyx fully clothed. The sight of On still dressed makes me feel cheap and used; bile threatens to rise in my throat. It burns as much as the tears pricking at the corner of my eyes.

What just happened? Everything was going so well... and now my three best friends in the world were suddenly at each other's throats and I'm huddled in a corner trying not to cry on my birthday. What the fuck?

This was such a bad idea. Not that it was an idea at all, really. It's not like I planned this - I may have fantasised about it for years - but I didn't set out to make this happen tonight. I wasn't thinking. And I should have.

You can't have sex with your best friend without something irrevocably changing. And I'd done that times three! Everything was so fucked up right now.

"Ru... Ru... RURI!" I'm so deeply wrapped in my despair and dismay that I don't notice Jasper calling me until he shouts. I look up and see him staring intently at me, kneeling right beside the sofa. Close enough that we could kiss. "You okay?" He asks and I shake my head no. I'm not okay. This is not okay.

"Stop fighting, please," I whisper. Jasper has to lean in close to hear me and his warm mix of sweet and spice scent fills me, comforts me, reminds me of home.

"Guys! Knock it off." Jasper turns and tells them, but stays by my side. Instantly, the room falls silent and Sterling and Onyx turn to face us. When Sterling sees how I'm sitting in his shirt, he pulls a face but doesn't say anything.

"We're sorry, Ru," Sterling tells me earnestly. "We

didn't mean for this to happen." The fighting or the sex, I wonder? "We weren't going to say anything," he continues, throwing a dirty look at Onyx. "But I guess some of us can't help ourselves."

"I've been patient enough," Onyx grumbles.

"What do you mean?" I ask softly.

"We agreed we weren't going to do this tonight, Ru," Sterling hesitates. Jasper slips onto the sofa beside me and pulls me onto his bare lap. I really wish I had my shorts on. This doesn't feel like a conversation I should be having half naked. Especially with a semi-hard cock pushing against my ass. Sterling takes a deep breath before continuing, "BUT, as Onyx has let the cat out of the bag anyway, we may as well be honest and lay all our cards out on the table."

"We're crazy about you, Ru. And we want to be more than just friends." Jasper interjects.

"We...?" My brows knit in confusion.

"All three of us." My eyes widen in shock at Sterling's emphatic statement.

"You...you can't mean that."

"They do. Which is why you're going to have to choose one of us." Onyx states. "You need to pick so that the other two can move on and get over it." There's something in the way he speaks that makes me think he's talking about Sterling and Jasper as 'the other two' - like he's *that* sure he'd be my choice. It gets my back up.

"I can't do that, guys," I say softly. "This, tonight, was a mistake. We shouldn't have done anything to make this awkward or to jeopardise our friendship. I couldn't be with one of you knowing how the other two feel. It wouldn't be right." I shake my head. "I can't lose any of you." I conclude sadly.

"You have to choose," Onyx insists at the same time as

Jasper says, "I'm so sorry we ruined your birthday." Jasper's words make my heart hurt while Onyx's make me angry.

"Did you stop to think about what this would do to our friendship, Onyx? Or how I might feel?" My voice trembles but I'm not about to cry. No, it's anger that's making me shake.

"Come off it, Ruri!" he scoffs. "Are you trying to tell me that you don't have feelings for me?"

"Of course I do! You're my best friend."

"Best friends? Ha! I don't make a habit of finger fucking my best friends!"

"Thankfully. I don't want your giant sausage digits poking up my ass," Sterling jokes, then hurries to add, "or any fingers for that matter!" It makes me smile despite the tension of the situation and I'm grateful that I can always rely on him for that.

I take a deep breath and realise that the only way out of this situation is by coming clean.

"Yes, you're right, Onyx," I say, and a triumphant gleam flashes through his eyes. "I do have feelings for you as more than a friend. I always have... but I also wouldn't have done any of that stuff with Jasper and Sterling either, if I didn't have feelings for them too."

"What are you saying?" The gleam has changed to a hard and challenging glint.

"I'm saying, I couldn't pick one of you to be with, because I'm in love with all three of you. And I always have been." I let my secret settle on the room like dust after a storm; slowly, but heavy with significance. The weight of my words, and knowing that I can't take them back, threatens to choke me. The urge to keep talking, to explain, to justify, fills me but I force myself to remain silent.

"What?" Onyx's mouth hangs open. He looks shell-shocked.

"Ru, are you sure?" Sterling asks.

"Pretty sure, yeah," I reply.

"Fuck." Jasper adds.

"Yeah. Everything's pretty fucked right now. Now do you understand why I can't choose... why I won't pick? Aside from ruining our friendships, it would tear me apart to have to say goodbye to two of you." Even the thought of it makes tears form in my eyes and Jasper wraps his arms around me and pulls me in tight for a hug.

"But...but..." Onyx stammers. If he didn't look so horrified, it would almost be funny. As it stands though, his expression shoots painful arrows at my heart.

"What if..." Sterling begins tentatively. "You didn't have to pick?"

"What do you mean?" I ask. What are they going to do, do shots to decide who gets to be with me instead of making me choose?

"What if..." he nibbles the corner of his lip unsure if he should continue.

"Just spit it out!" Onyx snaps.

"Okay! What if you were with all of us. What if...we...shared?"

Fuck! Excitement, hope, arousal flares through me at his suggestion. Jasper's cock fully hardens beneath me and jerks violently. I turn to him and smirk. "Do you like that idea, Jasp?"

"You know I do," he replies, kissing me on the nose. "There's no hiding it from you like this, is there?" We laugh.

"Is that a yes?" Sterling asks hopefully.

"It's not a no," I tell him before turning to Onyx and holding my breath. "On? What do you think?"

"How would it work?" He asks, unsure. I can see he's wavering, on the fence, but at least it wasn't an outright no.

"Honestly? I have no idea," I tell him earnestly. "But I'd like to try."

"Ru, I'm not sure." His eyes lock on mine and see his fear reflecting clearly in them. "What if it all blows up?"

"Isn't that a risk in any relationship?" I counter.

"Yeah, but with the potential to do three times the damage. Our friendship would be over."

"I think it's already irreparably damaged after tonight, On." I tell him softly. "I don't think I can go back to pretending I'm just your friend now that you know the truth."

"Besides," Jasper jumps in, "the way I see it, we have three times the incentive to make this relationship work, for the sake of *all* our friendships. Don't you agree?"

He has a point, so I nod.

"Look, can we sort out the finer details of this all tomorrow?" Sterling interjects.

"Why?" Jasper asks.

"Because..." he points at me. "Look at her! She's sat there, nearly naked but for my shirt, and something in me calls for me to make her mine!" He exclaims.

"Ours." Onyx growls.

"Yeah, that's what I meant." Sterling brushes him off. "So are we doing this?"

"Ru? What do you think?" Jasper turns to me. "Shall we finish your birthday with a real celebration?"

CHAPTER ELEVEN

Three sets of eyes stare intently at me and I'm not about to disappoint. I want them all - together at the same time. There's no way I'm turning this offer down.

"Okay," I nod, trying to act a little reluctant. "But Onyx has to take his clothes off."

"Get naked, dude!" Sterling hits him on the shoulder, but Onyx ignores him, frowning at me slightly.

"Why?" He gently challenges.

"Because you keeping your clothes on made me feel...bad." I finish lamely.

"Did it?" He steps closer to me, close enough that I can feel the heat of his body through the thin t-shirt I'm wearing. "At the time, when I was pounding in to you and the denim chafed against your spanked ass, did it feel...bad?"

Fuck no, it definitely didn't. I bite my lip as he presses himself against me. Shit, his words have the power to make me melt and drip faster than a church candle.

"And when I was buried up to my balls in your tight wet pussy, grinding against you so that the teeth on my zipper bit into your ass, did that feel...bad?"

"No! Okay! None of that stuff felt bad!" I cry reluctantly. I fan my face and lift the curls off the back of my neck. When did it get so hot in here? Onyx grabs my hair out of my hand, fists it, and kisses my exposed neck passionately.

"So you loved it while I was fucking you, but it was after that you felt 'bad' then?" He cocks his head to one side and studies me until I squirm. "Interesting... maybe you should think about that later." I scowl at him. I've no intention of doing anything later if I can help it. I'm ready to be screwed into oblivion.

Sterling approaches me and pulls me into a passionate kiss. It feels like he's claiming me, branding me as his. He pulls away and before I can catch my breath, Onyx grabs me to do the same. He bites down on my lip and I yelp into his mouth, but that doesn't deter him from devouring my mouth.

Jasper patiently waits his turn, but if I expected him to be more gentle with me, I was sorely mistaken. His kiss is...spectacular. Distracted, I barely notice that Sterling has removed his shirt from me and as the kiss ends, Onyx gently but firmly pushes me to my knees.

Eyes glued to mine, without blinking, Onyx slowly strips off his clothes until he's as breathtakingly naked as the others. Slowly, he approaches me and presents his cock to my lips.

I reach out and swirl my tongue around his balls before gently taking them into my mouth one at a time and sucking. I love the feel of my face buried into his crotch - pressed right up tight against his skin so that his neatly trimmed hair tickles my nose and restricts my breathing a little bit.

I tease his balls with my tongue, rolling and swirling them around and sucking smoothly. I love taking them both in my mouth at the same time and the full feeling of softness it brings.

His cock is dancing to get my attention now, jealous. I placate it as I work my way up and down the shaft with little licks and nibbles interspersed with feathery light kisses that I hope drive him wild. My hands cup his balls and gently fondle and squeeze them so that they remain in my attention too.

As I make my way back up his shaft once more, I cannot ignore his head any longer. I smile at my prize that rests, waiting patiently for me at the tip of his slit. I greedily lick at the glistening drop of pre-cum and then slide the head of his cock between my lips.

At first I just hold him there, trying to tease him a little, but it's no use - I love it - and so I soon start to swirl my tongue around his tip, rubbing my tongue against his frenulum and wiggling it inside his slit a little to try to tease out some more of that delicious pre-cum. I suck his head and enjoy the warmth it emits as he gets more turned on by me.

I remain where I am, lavishing attention on his head and playing with his balls until I feel his hand on the back of my head, firmly pushing me down deeper onto his shaft. As I open wide to take him, I can't help but smile at the way he takes control and forces me to give him what he wants.

While I'm administering to Onyx, Sterling comes behind me and gently lifts me up. Jasper slides under me, then Sterling replaces me on my knees so that I'm straddling Jasper.

Onyx pushes me all the way to the base of his shaft, stretching my jaw as wide as it can go, and then holds me there for a moment. At the same time, Jasper rubs his cock back and forth across my slit, my juices coating him and our thighs.

When acclimatised to Onyx's cock, he releases his hold on me so that I can draw myself back up his shaft to the tip before fractionally lowering myself back down. I love the tease - his groans of joy and frustration bring a gush of wetness between my legs - but it takes every ounce of self control not to start fucking him with my mouth.

I continue to slowly work my way up and down his shaft, rewarding him with kisses, licks and nibbles on his tip whenever his cock treats me to drops of delicious pre-cum. I groan when Jasper joins us and slips inside my wet pussy. When he starts to move, somehow in perfect tandem with Onyx, my eyes close in bliss. I clench my muscles to stave off the orgasm that threatens to spill already, desperate to wait for Sterling so that we can all be together, so that I can give myself to all of them equally.

Onyx fists his hands into my hair and pushes me right down onto his cock. Caught unaware, I cough and choke a little and his cock pulses even harder as it hits the back of my throat. He applies more pressure and when I gag a little he pushes through, past my defences, and enters my throat. His actions obviously turn Jasper on too, because he starts to fuck me hard, bouncing me up and down on his cock, while Onyx keeps my head clamped firmly in place around the bottom of his cock. I'm so close to coming it's unreal. I wish I could indicate to the guys somehow, but they have me trapped, powerless, and at their mercy.

The second Onyx releases me, I'm gulping and gasping for air. I look down through streaming eyes to see Jasper's hooded gaze blazing into mine. The arousal on his face nearly undoes me and I quickly lean forward to kiss him. He returns my passion equally and then clamps his hands around my elbows to hold me in place and to stop me from sitting back up.

I open my mouth to ask him what he's doing, but close it again when I feel Sterling pressing against my tightest hole. Oh! My eyes widen with shock and my heart rate increases with my nerves.

"Shh, it's ok Ru. Relax." Jasper whispers. "I've got you." I nod once and make a concentrated effort to relax my muscles. Jasper's hand stroking up and down my back helps me no end.

When I calm down a little, I notice that Sterling's cock is slick with lube. That helps, but as he pushes forward - oh so gently - my tight, muscular ring still fights his entrance. Whilst he's doing this, both Jasper and Onyx stop still and watch my every reaction.

I grit my teeth and hiss a little at the pain, but soon his cock is buried entirely in my ass. He holds still, allowing me to acclimatise, and that's when I notice that my pussy feels horribly empty. Jasper has slipped out, to allow me time to get used to Sterling, but now I want all of them.

Slowly, Jasper re-enters me, then him and Sterling begin to move together. My eyes flutter closed and roll back. A feeling of fullness I have never experienced in my life takes over and I wonder how I'll ever live without this now that I've been lucky enough to experience it.

"Open your eyes, Ru." Onyx demands and I have no choice but to obey. I lock eyes on him, silently begging him to join us once again. "Soon," he silently mouths to me.

My ass is rolling tightly up and down the full length of Sterling's cock as he slowly moves in and out, in direct opposition of Jasper's movements. It feels indescribably good, but I need more. I need Onyx.

"Please!" I gasp. "On!"

He doesn't disappoint. He sinks to his knees beside Jasper and helps me twist slightly so that I can reach his cock. He doesn't let me take control, beginning to fuck my throat with fervour, pulling me up just enough so that I can snatch little snippets of air from time to time before impaling me back down on his cock. The sounds of my struggles turn them all on more and I feel all of them grow and swell in my holes.

Jasper and Sterling find their rhythm, fucking me relentlessly. Sterling's grip on my hips digs deeply into my soft flesh. My cock-muffled grunts seem deafening to my ears. Combined with the sound of my ass slapping up and down on Jasper's lap, it's all I can do to maintain control.

Their powerful thrusts surge me forward onto Onyx's cock until it too is slamming into me. Tears glisten on my cheeks but the juices gushing from my pussy reveal how much I'm loving it.

"I'm going to cum, Ru. Get that cock down your throat to the base and keep it there until I've finished!" Ever obedient, I once again comply as Sterling gives one final thrust and holds himself balls-deep in my ass. Onyx's cock is balls-deep in my throat, and Jasper is fully sheathed inside my pussy too.

Everything inside me snaps; I can't help the powerful orgasm that overcomes me. With a wordless shout, all three of them empty spurt after spurt of red-hot cum deep inside of me.

My throat is raw. My jaw aches. My eyes are streaming. My nose is running. My hair and makeup is a mess. My lungs are screaming. But I wouldn't have it any other way.

Finally Onyx releases me, pulling sharply upwards on my hair so that he's ejected from my mouth suddenly and I am gasping, coughing and crying as I fight for air. Some of his cum covers my face - hot and thick - and he uses his hand to pinch my clit sending me reeling over the edge and into another delicious orgasm.

"Beautiful!" He smiles down on me. "Now clean up the mess you've made, Ru!"

I'm only too happy to oblige.

EPILOGUE

"Fuck that was amazing!" Sterling exclaims.

"Totally worth waiting for!" Jasper agrees.

"I want to do it again!" I add.

"Jesus Ru, give me a minute to recover." Sterling grumbles and I laugh.

"I didn't mean right away." I clarify, "I just meant, I want to do it again, in my lifetime. Preferably quite soon, after some food and some sleep."

Throughout this exchange, Onyx has been deathly quiet. I turn to him with trepidation and ask tentatively, "On? You okay?"

"Hmm? Oh yeah, I'm fine." He states distractedly.

"Was it...okay?" I probe.

"Of course!" He's not giving much away. I don't know if I should be annoyed or worried.

"And do you think you'd want to do this again?" I gnaw on my bottom lip nervously.

"Absolutely! I want my turn in your other holes!" He laughs.

"Asshole!" I hiss.

"Yeah and your pussy." He quips.

"You already had that." I point out, sticking my tongue out at him playfully.

"Not while you were being filled and gagged by my best mate's cocks." He tells me. As sore and exhausted as I am, his words still have the power to make my pussy clench.

"So you just want me for the sex?" I challenge, hands on hips.

"No, Ru. I'm teasing. That was amazing. I wasn't sure how it was going to work, being all together like that. But it was hands down the best sex I've ever had, and I'm not giving that up for anything!"

"So it *is* just about the sex then," I demand.

"Hush, silly. I thought I might feel jealous and not want to share you. I assumed you'd have to pick one of us..."

"But...?" I prompt when he infuriatingly stops.

"But once I saw how happy you were with the three of us, I realised how much better this is. With all of us."

"So...?" I feel like I'm trying to get blood out of a stone. Ugh! Just tell me already, I want to cry.

"So I'm asking, Ruri...will you be my - our - girlfriend and allow us to be lucky enough to share you?"

I giant smile splits my face in two and I launch myself at the three men with the power to simultaneously make all my dreams come true. "Yes!" I cry in elation as I lose myself in their warm embrace.

"We should celebrate!" Sterling announces.

"I thought you needed a minute to recover?" I ask.

"I meant with food!"

"Best. Idea. Ever." I reply.

"No Ru, I think our game of Trick or Treat was the best idea ever," Onyx says with a wink.

I smile at him, at them all, and agree. This has turned

out to be the best Halloween - the best birthday - ever. The guys have managed to give me all the happy, shiny, glossy, glittery, fluttery feelings in the world. And I couldn't be happier.

"So...food? What do you fancy?" Sterling asks. My three best friends - boyfriends - stare at me.

"Don't look at me, you know I can't choose!"

A note from the author

Hey, thank you so much for reading 'Trick of Treat'. I hope you enjoyed it as much as I enjoyed writing it.

I'd absolutely love to know your thoughts about this story, so please consider taking time to leave me a review on Amazon or Goodreads. I really appreciate it, and it helps to spread the word to other like-minded readers who might enjoy this book. You can be as brief as you like, I don't mind, I just love the feedback!

If you haven't already, please check out my first full-length RH novel, Vengeance. The reviews so far have been amazing, and this is my absolute book baby - the story I want to share with the world.

ABOUT THE AUTHOR

Crystal North is now a full time romance author, after finally leaving education for good. As well as writing, she's looking after her savage preschooler, her man-child husband, their needy fur baby and her many houseplants, pet rocks and shiny crystals. She likes to read dark, twisty, stabby, steamy books, and dream up wicked new cliffhangers to torture her readers with. And if she ever finds herself with free time, she spends it reading her never ending TBR pile.

https://www.crystalnorthauthor.com

Read all the books

Santa Catalina University Series

Silenced

Endangered

Exposed

Revered

The Holy Trinity (Part of The Black Hallows Saga)

Hunting Grounds

Hunting Games

Hunting Graves - Coming Soon

Knox Academy (The Order World)

F*ck You: Knox Academy: Term 1

F*ck off: Knox Academy: Term 2

F*ck Yeah : Knox Academy: Easter Break

F*ck Her: Knox Academy: Term 3

Vengeance Series (Part of The Order World)

Vengeance

Atonement

Retribution

Lizzie's Story - coming soon

All That Remains (Part of The Order World)

Fractured Remains

Shattered Remains

Unbroken Remains - coming soon

Jewels Cafe/ Spell Library / Silver Skates Shared World

Jasmine

Lumi

Standalones

Branding Belle

Frozen in time

Bearing the Curse

Her Christmas Wish

Trick or Treat

Bosses' Brat

Printed in Great Britain
by Amazon

42855263R00051